SPRING BREAK

PETER LERANGIS

AN
APPLE
PAPERBACK

To Alex,
Zach, and their parents!
Love,
Uncle Peter

SCHOLASTIC INC.
New York Toronto London Auckland Sydney

To Nancy Hall,
for taking a chance

ISBN 0-590-69771-4

12 11 10 9 8 7 6 5 4 3 2 1   6 7 8 9/9 0 1/0

Printed in the U.S.A.   40

First Scholastic printing, April 1996

1
The *D* Word

"**S**woke foo!" I called out.

I had meant to say "Strike three!" My best friend, Shawn Ferguson, had just struck out against my new pitching machine. But I couldn't quite get the words out. My mouth was full of double chocolate chocolate chip toffee mint crunch ice cream bar.

"Whaaaat?" Shawn said. "That was below my knees! You're blind as a bat, Adam."

"No, it's just the blubber deposits on his eyelids," said my sister, Rachel. "They're distorting his vision."

"Hey, no insulting the ump!" I said. "If this were a real game, I could throw you out!"

"If this were a real game," Rachel replied, "it would be called on account of a beached whale on the field. Come on, Shawn, load up the machine and try again."

A beached whale? She was asking for it. I couldn't let her get away with that comment. No, sir. I had to come back with something sharp. Something cruel. Something that would really knock her off her feet.

"Dork!" I shouted.

Rachel groaned. "Real clever, Adam. Wow, I don't know how you thought of that one."

I shut my mouth while I was behind.

I hate having a genius for a sister. She's only nine, but she has enough IQ points for three people. At least that's what her teachers say. They treat her as if she's Einstein or something.

Frankenstein is more like it, if you ask me.

I, Adam Fenster, am more the strong, silent type. Well, maybe not that strong. I came in last in the Hopnoodle Middle School physical fitness exam.

Maybe not that silent, either, except when I'm eating. Which is most of the time.

I love food. All kinds, too, not just ice cream. I like pizza, cheeseburgers, bacon, peanut butter and jelly sandwiches, crackers, chicken nuggets, marshmallows, pork roast, soft pretzels, really really sweet fruit . . . I could go on, but I'd start to drool all over the page.

The trouble is, I eat when I'm happy. I also eat when I'm sad. I guess if I didn't sleep, I'd eat all the time. I just can't help it.

I've always been like that. Mom says my first word was "Mouth." When I was a toddler, I tried to eat wet cement at one of my dad's construction sites. I thought it was oatmeal.

I'd love to be thin and muscular. I've tried. I once replaced lunch with this muscle-building powdered drink Mom got at a health-food store. It didn't work.

My dad's always hinting I should cut back. Rachel calls me an equal opportunity pig.

Good old Mom refuses to call me fat or piggy or obese or dumpling-shaped or husky or any of those words. She lets me devour whatever I want. She says it's bad to stigmatize children. I heartily agree.

Now I just have to find out what *stigmatize* means.

Not many families could afford to feed me. Including us, back when Dad's construction company was almost defunct.

Yep, it's true. We weren't always rich. In fact, if you'd told Dad back then he'd be founder and C.E.O. of a famous real estate empire, he'd have laughed in your face.

But of course, you know our rags-to-riches story. You've heard all about it on tabloid TV. About this strange family, the Ghieks, who transformed Hopnoodle Village from a dinky little ooga-horn-manufacturing town to the cool place it is now. I won't go into that, but Shawn could tell you all about it. He claims the Ghieks were alien beings, but he can be a little weird.

Anyway, Dad's business took off. Fenster Contracting became the famous Fensterworks International, Ltd.

Being the son of a world-class tycoon is kind of fun. First of all, kids don't tease me as much about my weight as they used to. Second, I have the coolest house in town. It has thirty-seven rooms and it's modeled after some English castle, complete with a moat and drawbridge. We added some classy modern stuff, too, like a rooftop mirror ball that reflects moonlight onto the yard in electric colors. Also, all our doors inside are voice-activated. My bedroom door opens at the sound of a deep belch that only I can do. (Way too deep for Rachel to imitate, so she can't come in.)

My favorite part of the house is our yard. It has a man-made lake, a pool, a horse pasture, and a major-league-sized baseball field.

No, I'm not a baseball fan. I hate playing sports, to tell you the truth. Dad had the field built because he thought he'd make an athlete out of me (ha ha). I don't mind umpiring, though. Especially on a warm spring day, stretched out on a beach chair, eating ice cream, with my handy motorized freezer at my side.

As Shawn gathered up the baseballs and dropped them into the pitching machine, I finished my ice cream bar and took another one out of my freezer. I was thirsty, so I squeezed my gold-plated ooga horn to summon our butler, Beauregard. (Yes, butler. Don't be too jealous.)

AH-*OOOOO*-GAHHHH!

"What now?" grumbled Beauregard, trudging out of the house.

I held out my Hopnoodle Hornblowers baseball team cup. "Beau, could you please refresh my sport drink?"

"It's 'Mr. Tutweiler,' to you," he muttered.

"Sure, Beau," I replied. "And maybe you could bring a fruit bowl with some sherbet? You know, to cleanse the palate?" (I don't know what that means, but Mom always says that when she serves fruit.)

Beau's lips curled into a sneer. "Yes, my liege."

I like Beau. He's funny.

Don't worry, I don't rank on him too much. I feel kind of bad for him. Working for our family is not exactly the highlight of his life. He used to have a good job in the neighboring town, Pifflethorn; it went down the tubes a while back. Nowadays, Beau lives with his wife and his son, Buford, in a little development called Fensterville.

"Shawn, try choking up on the bat," I suggested, biting into a frozen Snickers bar.

"What do you mean?" Shawn asked. (He's even a worse athlete than I am.)

"Like this." I leaned forward to demonstrate. But a nut from the Snickers bar caught in my throat. I dropped the bar and started gagging. My eyes bugged out.

Shawn studied my reaction for a moment. Then he started gagging, too.

"Not that kind of choking, Shawn!" Rachel said. "MO-O-OM! DA-A-AD!"

My mother came racing out of the house. Her jewelry was jangling around her neck. Her hairdo, which looks like a small mountain, was swaying from side to side.

"Adam, dear, are you all right?" she cried.

I would have been fine, if Shawn hadn't been pounding my back like a tom-tom. I swallowed my Snickers and yelled, "Yo, knock it off!"

Out of the corner of my eye, I spotted Rachel picking up the baseball bat. She activated the pitching machine and took a swing.

SMMMMMMACK!

Doesn't it figure? She's barely big enough to hold the bat, but the ball went on a line drive right to the house.

It crashed through the bay window of my dad's conference room.

Our alarm system started blaring — sirens and whistles and a deafening digital voice that shouts: *"HOW DARE YOU? DO YOU KNOW WHOSE HOUSE THIS IS?"*

Rachel was screaming with glee. Shawn was whacking me so hard, I thought I'd throw up.

Mom had her cellular phone all tangled up in her hairdo, trying to call 911.

And now my dad was rushing out of the house. Behind him, the officials of the Hopnoodle Civic Association were staring at me, totally bewildered.

I pushed Shawn away. I hoisted myself to my feet. I prepared to run for my life. When Dad gets mad, it's not a pretty sight.

But he was smiling ear to ear. "What a shot!" he called out. "That's my boy! Did you see that, fellas?"

"*I* hit that, Daddy!" Rachel announced.

"We-e-e-ell, uh, very nice, dear," Dad said. "I'm sure your brother was a fine coach."

"No way. He was sitting on his butt the whole time, eating ice cream."

Dad's smile disappeared.

It was coming. I could smell it. The Lecture. The *Why-can't-you-stop-eating-and-be-a-normal-skinny-ballplaying-kid-like-everyone-else?* speech.

I tried to kick my ice cream bar wrapper under the beach chair and out of sight. Good old Shawn put his foot over the half-eaten Snickers bar.

"Adam," Dad said under his breath, "you disgrace the Fenster name."

"But Dad," Rachel countered, "you told us our ancestors were all horse thieves."

"Precisely!" Dad replied. "And what successful

7

horse thief ever had a bloated belly and slow reflexes?"

"Orvis, please," Mom whispered to Dad, "don't make a scene in front of your committee."

At that moment, Beau came trundling over with a rolling cart, loaded up with bananas, grapes, cantaloupe, pineapple, and sherbet. "Dessert, Your Pudginess?" he snarled.

I made an urgent face at him. A face that said *TAKE THAT AWAY*.

Too late. Dad was staring at the cart. "Fruit?" he said. "Hmm. Very healthy. You like fruit, Adam?"

"Yes!" I blurted. "Very much, Dad."

Dad grinned. "Good. Because from now on, that's all you're going to eat. Fruit and vegetables. I'm putting you on a diet, young man."

I staggered back. I felt faint. Never in my life has anyone in my family spoken the dreaded *D* word.

"But Dad —"

"Orvis," Mom said, "he's a growing boy."

"You can say that again," Rachel mumbled.

But Dad's eyes were on fire. And I knew that look well. The last time I saw it, he built me a gym with weight machines and hired a personal trainer. It was the low point of my entire life.

"Well, it's time he stopped growing," Dad said. "Maybe he'll even shrink a little." He turned to

Beauregard. "Beau, would you cancel our Disney World vacation plans?"

"Yep," Beau grunted.

"Cancel?" I shouted. "But why?"

"Because," Dad said calmly, "you, Adam Fenster, are going to spend spring break in a health spa. You will work out, eat practically nothing, and mold yourself into a man!"

My jaw hit the ground.

Rachel cackled. "A fat farm, a fat farm. Adam's going to a fat farm!"

"And," Dad continued, "we're going with you."

Rachel dropped her bat. Mom's hairdo sagged.

I felt the corners of my mouth turn up weakly. "A joke, right, Dad?" I squeaked.

Dad shook his head. "I'm dead serious. And maybe if we all set an example for you, *you'll* be serious, too."

I gulped. I turned. I walked slowly into the house, toward my room. I belched my door open. I held it for Shawn, who had followed me all the way. I closed the door behind me.

Coolly, calmly, I sat on my bed.

Then I screamed my guts out.

2
Buford's Bright Idea

"**P**ut that chocolate pudding back, Adam Fenster!"

The words sent a chill up my spine.

I stared into the cold, stern eyes of Ms. Glupe, the Hopnoodle Middle School lunch lady. Her fingers were firmly around my wrist.

It was Monday, a full day after my horrible punishment. For twenty-four hours, I had eaten nothing but the healthiest, most nutritious food provided by Mother Nature. No refined sugars, no fats, nothing fried. I thought I was going to die.

Now my hands were shaking. The pudding — that luscious, quivering glob of glorious sweetitude — was at arm's length. Its chocolately aroma was dancing around my nostrils.

"But — but —" I protested.

"Don't *but* me, young man," Ms. Glupe said. "Did you think your parents would neglect to call the school cafeteria?"

The pudding jiggled one last time as I set it down. I almost choked on the drool I had to suck back into my mouth.

I took a carrot salad and slid my tray down the line toward Shawn.

Unfortunately, Buford Tutweiler had slipped into the line behind me. Buford used to be my archenemy. Now that his dad works for mine, he's worse.

"Mmmmmm, chocolate pudding!" he cried. "That'll go nicely with my butterscotch Heath Bar crunch ice cream sundae. Oh, and this banana cream pie looks tasty, too."

The words were like knives in my back. I was weak. My knees were giving out.

"Don't listen to him, Adam," Shawn said. "And don't look back. Just follow me. Understand?"

Half blind with hunger, I walked into the lunch room.

Shawn had selected some healthy stuff, too, to make me feel better. We sat at a table, our bowls of lettuce and fruit staring up at us defiantly. Daring us to eat them.

"Guess what?" Shawn said. "My mom and dad said I could come with you."

"Where?" I asked, my throat parched with hunger.

"On your trip," Shawn said. "Remember? Over spring break?"

I had almost forgotten. "To the fat farm, you mean."

"Health resort," Shawn corrected me. "Do you think your parents will let me?"

"If you agree to eat crabgrass and run a marathon."

"Heeyyyy, anybody sitting next to you two natural food dudes?"

It figured. Of all the tables in the cafeteria, Buford would have to pick ours.

"Cram it, Buford," Shawn said. "Go sit with someone your own IQ."

"Don't worry, I don't mind lowering myself," Buford replied. He plopped down in the seat across from me and shoveled a spoonful of ice cream sundae into his mouth. "Mmmmmmm. Flavorful."

Shawn had to hold me back. *"Look away,"* he said through clenched teeth.

"So," Buford said, "find a good fat farm yet?"

"How — who told you — ?" I sputtered.

"My dad. Or Beau, as you call him." Buford pulled a folded glossy magazine page out of his pocket. "But hey, have no fear, Buford's here. I cut out some ads from the Sunday news magazine. Check these out."

He handed the sheet to me. On top, a headline said SPECIAL RESORTS AND CAMPS/SPRING SESSION ACTIVITIES. Underneath were all these dorky-looking photos of thin guys holding out the waists of their huge pants.

"For a small fee," Buford continued, "I can serve as your booking agent. I'll research the coolest places —"

"Guess again, Buford." I crumpled the sheet up and looked around for the trash can.

"Fine," Buford said with a shrug. "Let your dad pick where you go. Doesn't matter to me. Just trying to help."

I stopped. Buford had a point. If I left it up to Dad, I might be spending spring break in Siberia.

I smoothed out the sheet. "What did you have in mind?"

Buford leaned over and breathed his sundae right into my face. Then he pointed to an ad in the center of the page. "How about this one: 'Yo, come to Phat-Phree Pharm, where kids rap themselves to recovery! Let those newly baggy pants become attractive hip hop fashion accessories!' "

I gave Buford a look.

"No, huh? Okay, how about 'Waist Land — for the ingestionally challenged, in an environmentally conscious setting.' Uh-uh. Um, let's see . . . 'Belly Busters, spring session'? 'The Slim Gym, for Her and Him'? At least there'll be girls there. That's important."

I groaned. "I don't believe this."

Buford turned the page over. "Here's one: 'Fulfill Your Deepest Wish. Make Your Dreams Come True. Spend a week, a month, a lifetime at our beautiful amusement park and spa, the Dreamworld Health and Fitness Resort for Seniors, near historic Mashpea Swamp.' Sounds perfect!"

"Yeah, perfect for *seniors*, you doof," I said. "I hate to break this to you, but I'm in seventh grade, like you."

"How many times were you left back?" Buford asked.

"Once!" I retorted. "And only because I kept eating the art supplies in kindergarten!"

"Okay, so technically you're in eighth. You were born in January, which gives you almost another year. And a lot of seniors graduate early, and you're actually only two years behind them, which puts you virtually in tenth grade — plus you're big for your age. You can pass, no sweat!" Buford shoved some more sundae into his mouth. "And just imagine what the girls will be like there!"

I couldn't follow that. But it seemed to make sense.

"Dreamworld does sound better than the others," Shawn said.

"I guess," I grumbled.

"You're welcome!" Buford said brightly. "So, rich boy, are your dad and mom going to take along an assistant?"

"Yeah, your dad, as usual," I said.

Buford downed his pudding, then licked the

bowl clean. "Bad choice. He'll really make you stick to your diet."

"Do you have any other suggestions?" Shawn asked.

Buford grinned. "I, Buford, own a twenty-three pocket safari suit, ideal for the smuggling of small, wrapped, chocolate objects. Plus, I'd rather spend spring break around the pool with senior girls than with my parents in Fensterville. And I know my dad wouldn't mind a break from you, no offense."

"Take *you* along?" I was flabbergasted. "The ad says *dreams* come true, not nightmares!"

"You drive a hard bargain, Fenster." Buford sighed. "All right, I'll throw in travel arrangements, too."

"Thanks, but no thanks." I grabbed my tray and stood up.

"Not so fast." Buford pointed his chocolate-and-saliva-smeared spoon at me. "As I see it, you have two choices. Choice number one is going home and discussing the options with your dad over a dinner of white rice and steamed asparagus."

"And choice number two?" I asked.

"My house, after school," Buford replied. "We make the arrangements ourselves, before your dad even tries."

"I can't do that! He'd kill me!"

"Leave it to me," Buford said. "I'll make your dad thank you."

"Come on, Shawn," I called. "Let's go."

"I have three fresh pints of Ben and Jerry's ice cream in my freezer," Buford blurted out. "What does your dad have in yours?"

The answer? Frozen brussels sprouts and tofu casserole. I'd seen Mom sneaking it in.

"Okay, it's a deal," I said.

"Adam!" Shawn protested.

I held out my hand.

Instead of shaking it, Buford dug out a small pile of Heath Bar Crunch ice cream and handed the spoon to me.

I have never tasted anything better in my whole life.

3
The Plot

"**R**ainforest Crunch, New York Super Fudge Chunk, or Cherry Garcia?" Buford asked.

Just hearing the choices was making me dizzy.

"Yes," I said.

Buford plopped the cartons on his kitchen table. Shawn glanced at his watch. "Okay . . . go!"

I ripped the cover off the Rainforest Crunch. I shoved the ice cream in so fast my head was aching. When I was finished I dropped the empty carton on the table. "Done!"

Shawn was looking at me with admiration. "Forty-seven seconds. A new record."

"Awesome," said Buford. "Now let's get to business."

By the time he brought the phone to the table, I'd finished the other two pints.

I was refreshed and ready. I picked up the receiver and tapped out the phone number in the ad: 1-800-DREAM ON.

"Hellllo-o-o-o," said a deep, laid-back voice.

"Dreamworld Resort for Seniors, Mr. Binglehausen speaking. How can I help make your dream come true?"

"Uh, I'd like to make a reservation." I reached into my pocket for a Fensterworks International credit card, which Dad lets me use. "Seven days, during spring break."

"Spring break?" said the voice. "Are you a senior?"

Oops. I must have sounded too young.

I harrumphed, then lowered my voice. "Uh, yeah. I have a cold."

"I see. So tell me, ma'am, what is your deepest desire? Has your step lost that old spring, is the ticker not what it used to be — ?"

"Ma'am?" I blurted out. "I mean, *man!* Man, do I need a vacation."

"Bully for you!" the voice said. "You won't even know yourself by the time you leave. *If* you leave. Now, will this be for one, or is there a special someone coming along?"

If you leave?

"Uh, well, yeah. I mean, no. My whole family is going. Four. Plus two friends. So that's, um . . . "

Shawn scribbled *Six* on the notepad by the phone.

"Six," I said confidently.

Buford was pumping his fist in the air. Shawn was doing a little victory dance.

Sure they were happy. I'd just handed them a free vacation. Behind Dad's and Mom's backs.

What was I doing?

"Excuse me," I grumphed. Then I covered the receiver and hissed, *"I can't do this! Dad'll disown me!"*

"I *said* I'd take care of it!" Buford said. "Trust me."

I closed my eyes. I unwrapped my fingers from the receiver.

Quickly I gave Mr. Binglehausen the dates of spring break and Dad's Fensterworks credit card number.

"Very good," the man said. "I look forward to seeing you, Mrs. Fensterworks."

"Yo, who are you calling — ? I — I mean, someone's calling! Gotta go."

Click.

Shawn let out a whoop. "You did it!"

"The guy was totally weird," I said, pacing the kitchen. "The place is probably a loony bin. Dad's going to hit the roof —"

"If he gives you trouble," Buford said, "call me. I'll cover."

"Thanks a lot," I said. "I feel about as safe as a lit match in a firecracker shop."

"Heyyyyy, relax, dude," Buford said. "From now on, you're on my team."

Shawn and I exchanged a look.

Maybe a fat farm wouldn't have been such a bad idea, after all.

That night, Mom served us ground-up frogs with cream sauce for dinner. At least that's what it looked like.

"What *are* those things?" Rachel asked.

"Spinach croquettes," Mom explained.

I thought I was going to lose my Rainforest Crunch.

"Looks delightful," said Dad.

"May I be excused?" Rachel asked. "I'm feeling sick."

As she staggered away from the table, I bolted up from my seat. "Me, too. I think I ate too much ice cr — uh, iceberg lettuce."

"Sit, Adam!" Dad ordered.

"Orvis, he's not a pet," Mom scolded.

"I'm sorry," Dad said. "Listen, Adam, I want to apologize for being so gruff yesterday. Maybe I was being rash about my decision for spring break."

"No problem, Dad." I plunged my fork into the glop. Green liquid oozed out and I almost gagged. "Actually, I've been thinking a lot about what you said. And you know what? I decided you were right."

Dad looked totally thunderstruck. "You did?"

Say it, Adam! my inner self screamed.

20

"Yep," I replied. "I even called a health spa and made a reservation for us."

I took a deep breath. I prepared for the atomic blast.

"What health spa?" Dad asked.

I stood up and got ready to run for cover. "Dreamworld. Mashpea Swamp. Amusement park and spa. One-eight-hundred-DREAM ON. Reservation for six. I invited Buford and Shawn, too."

There. I said it.

"Sit!" Dad shouted.

I plopped in my chair.

"Eat," Mom pleaded.

I stuffed a hunk of croquette in my mouth. Maybe they'd take pity on me if I developed food poisoning.

"Why didn't you consult us?" Mom asked. "This isn't like you, Adam."

I wanted to reply. But I couldn't. The glob was stuck. I felt as if I had a basketball in my throat. I closed my eyes and gulped.

Have you ever eaten a spinach croquette? Take my advice. Don't. It tastes like congealed slime.

"GAAAAWWWW!" I said.

"Excuse me, dear?" Mom asked.

"Good!" I said. "Those are good."

Mom stood up. "I'll get you some more."

Dad stood up. "I think I'll call this Dreamworld place."

I stood up. *"NO-O-O!"*

Mom and Dad both stared at me.

"I mean, WHO-O-OA, I'm full. Thanks, Mom."

Buford's words came back to me. *If your dad gives you trouble, call me.* I leaped across the room and grabbed the phone. "Let me get them for you, Dad."

"But I can —" Dad protested.

I tapped out the Tutweilers' phone number.

"That you, Fenster?" said Buford's voice.

"Uh . . . uh . . . hello, Dreamworld?" I said. "This is Mr. Fenster speaking. The son."

Buford cackled. "I knew it! I knew it! Okay, here goes." He put on a grumbly, grown-up voice. (He can do that much better than I can.) "The son of the world-famous Orvis Fenster? How is he? Can't wait to meet him!"

"Thank you, Mr. Binkledoozer. My world-famous father is just fine, and he's looking forward to meeting you, too. In fact, he'd like to talk to you."

Dad was beaming as I handed him the phone.

I prayed. If Buford blew it, I was in the doghouse.

"Yes, Fenster here," Dad said. "I believe there's been some mistake. My son is only thirteen . . . yes, yes, I am the fellow you saw in the papers. . . . Sure, I'm interested." Slowly his eyes lit up. "Is that a fact? Really? Well, all right. Yes, I'm looking forward to meeting you, too, sir."

When Dad hung up, he was grinning ear to ear. I swallowed hard. "What did he tell you?"

"He said he's been following my career," Dad replied. "And he'd be proud to sell me the entire resort if we all came down. At a bargain price."

"Whaaaaat?" I said.

Dad slapped me on the back. "That's my boy, Adam. You really know how to pick them!"

4
Spring Break

"**A**lo-o-o-o-ha-a-a o'eeee!"

I awoke to a strange, tortured bellowing. My eyes sprang open. I leaped out of bed.

Quickly I looked at my desk clock. Six A.M.

Slowly reality sank in. It was the second Saturday in April.

The first day of spring break.

"ALO-O-O-O-HA-A-A O'EEEE!"

The bellowing was coming nearer. I stepped backward in fear and fell onto my bed.

Unfortunately I'd left my door cracked overnight. It swung open.

"RISE AND SHIIIIINE!"

The creature in front of me looked like my father. It had his height. His big jiggly pot belly. His pale white skin and saggy jowls.

But the huge thatched-straw hat on its head was like nothing I'd ever seen on this planet. It looked like someone's taco salad that had been smashed and left to harden for a month.

The leather sandals exposed a set of toes that looked as if they'd been through a trash compactor. And the orange, red, and purple Hawaiian shirt was so loud I had to shield my eyes.

"Dad?" I asked.

"Hi! It's our first day of vacation. This is my son, Adam, greeting the new day with glee in his heart. Say good morning, Adam."

I couldn't believe it. Dad was videotaping me!

"Uh . . . uh . . . 'morning," I mumbled.

"Next we go to the breakfast table, where my daughter Rachel is eating a wholesome meal, looking forward to the long car ride ahead . . . "

I reached under my bed. I shook the dust bunnies off a pair of underwear, a shirt, and some shorts.

In minutes I was dressed and downstairs.

When I hit the kitchen, I froze. A goopy tune was playing on Dad's favorite radio station, KCORN, and Mom and Dad were dancing near the stove. Mom was shimmying around in a big, ugly dress that matched Dad's ensemble, holding a spatula in her right hand. Dad's Hawaiian shirt was riding upward, exposing a ring of belly flab that looked like an enormous uncooked bagel.

"What is going on?" I asked.

Rachel shrugged. "I can't be responsible for them."

"Ah, Fred, you're so debonair!" Mom sighed.

Dad laughed. "Nonsense, Ginger!"

Fred and Ginger? They looked more like sumo wrestlers.

I scooted around them and grabbed a bowl from the cupboard.

Have I mentioned we were only allowed to eat one kind of cereal? It's made of seventeen grains, has no sugar, no fat, no taste, and is called Pure 'n' Wholesome All Over. (I call it Puke 'n' Belch 'Em All Over.)

Ding-dong!

I forced down a spoonful of cereal and bolted. "I'll get it!"

I pulled open the door. It was Beauregard and Buford Tutweiler. "We have arrived, Your Wideness," grumbled Beau.

I let them in. Beau trundled off to the kitchen to report for work, but Buford and I hung back.

"Well?" I said.

Buford pulled open his safari jacket. "Three Musketeers, Skor, Milky Way, or Mars?"

Saved! I let my fingers do the talking. They pulled out a Mars and a Skor bar. I quickly tore off the wrappers and gobbled the candy down.

"Ahhh," I sighed.

"A 'thank you' would be nice," Buford said.

"Hey, guys!" shouted Shawn's voice behind us.

The Fergusons' car was parked in front, behind the Tutweilers'. Shawn and his parents were walking up the front path, lugging suitcases.

I licked the chocolate stains off my teeth. "Hi!"

"And here are Shawn and Buford, two of Adam's middle school buddies!" Dad announced, stalking toward us with his camcorder.

Buford started scratching his head and making monkey noises. His safari jacket flew open. I could see little candy wrapper tops flapping.

I leaped in front of him. "Uh, ha ha. Isn't Buford funny? We sure are excited about our trip."

Shawn cracked up. (Okay, so I'm not going to be an actor when I grow up.)

Mr. Ferguson, who happens to be the mayor of Hopnoodle Village, stepped in front of all of us. "On behalf of the Ferguson family and our fair village itself, I just want to express a few word of thanks to my good friend Orvis . . . "

While he was yammering, I pulled Buford toward the kitchen, grabbing two Milky Way bars from his inner pocket. I dropped the wrappers in my cereal bowl, then dumped the contents into the trash.

Rachel was watching me, her mouth open (which, full of chewed-up cereal, was not too attractive). "I'm telllling!" she said.

Buford tossed her a Snickers. "Try it, and that's the last one you'll ever see."

Rachel grumbled as she scarfed it down. Beauregard Tutweiler grumbled as he lugged my suitcase through the kitchen, on the way out the back door. Buford grumbled that his supply was already half gone.

Me? I wasn't grumbling at all. Neither was my happy stomach.

Many hugs, kisses, and sappy good-byes later, we climbed into the family limo. As our chauffeur, Cheevers, loaded the luggage into the trunk, we all shouted more good-byes out the window.

Everyone was teary-eyed, except Buford's parents. I actually saw them clicking their heels as the limo pulled away.

"Fasten your seatbelts and shoulder harnesses," Mom nagged.

"Here we are, riding down Fenster Boulevard on a beeeee-oot-ee-ful morning . . . " Dad said, pointing his camera out the window.

"I'm hungry!" Rachel whined.

"I know a great car game!" Shawn shouted.

"Do you guys have extra bags?" Buford asked. "Not that I get carsick too regularly, but just in case."

"*I'm not sitting next to him!*" Rachel screamed.

"Sit down!" Mom cried.

"Now we're crossing South Main Street . . . " Dad intoned. "Hello, city hall! See you again in a week!"

The car went over a bump. Buford's face turned slightly green. "Uh, by the way, c-could you, um, open a window?" he said.

I buried my head in my hands.

This was going to be some spring break.

5
The Journey

"**I** packed my bag and in it I put . . . " I muttered.
Everyone was staring at me. (That's the only thing I don't like about limos. You all sit facing each other in the back, so kids can't really fool around.)

I hated Shawn's car game. Everyone had to add one ingredient to the "I packed my bag" list — but you had to remember every item each player had said before you.

"He forgot everything already!" Rachel taunted.

"Did not!" I began reciting: "Um, a gallon of rocky road ice cream, a Barbie doll with a brain, an alien-finder kit, a million-dollar check addressed to B. Tutweiler, a copy of *Mothers Are People, Too*, a United States savings bond . . . "

(Can you figure out who'd put in what? Duh.)

"And a gallon of mint chocolate chip ice cream," I added.

"That's the same thing you picked before!" Rachel said.

"Different flavor!" I retorted.

"Cheater, cheater, piggy eater!" Rachel sang.

"Rachel, dear, Adam's been very good about his diet," Mom said.

"Oh, yeah, then how come his belly's the same size?" Rachel asked with a smirk.

"Just take your turn, dweeb face," I said.

"Ahem." Rachel rattled off all the ingredients and added, "A bulky safari jacket that has a suspicious sweet smell, because it's full of —"

Yikes.

"Shawn's turn!" I blurted out.

Shawn instantly changed the topic. "Uh, I forgot everything. Rats, I lose, game's over. Hey, let's play the license game. Our state doesn't count."

"Boring," Rachel said. "Mom, I'm hungry."

Mom reached into the limo's tiny refrigerator. "I packed a tuna fish and banana sandwich for you."

Rachel's face lit up. "My favorite!"

I told you she was weird.

Rachel peeled off the tin foil from her sandwich, filling the car with a horrible stench.

"Is there an exhaust fan in here?" I asked.

"Ohhhhh . . ." Buford groaned.

Shawn pointed out the window. "I see a New Jersey plate!"

"No, dassh Rhode I-lump," Rachel mumbled,

spitting brownish-yellow bits of tuna and banana.

"Say it, don't spray it," I said.

"*Ohhhhh* . . ." Buford was turning green. "I don't feel good."

Mom's face went pale. "Cheevers, dear, do you have a motion sickness receptacle?"

"You mean, a barf bag?" Cheevers asked.

"And the red car is Delaware," Rachel rattled on, "and there's Georgia, and Michigan . . ." She stopped and took another bite. "Ooooh, Kentucky!"

As the *tuck* of *Kentucky* left her mouth, so did a moist hunk of sandwich.

"Glub."

Well, that was more or less what Buford said. His hands shot up to his mouth and his eyes bugged out.

Dad yelped and lifted his camcorder away from Buford.

"EEEEEEWWWWWW! Rachel dropped her sandwich and started shrieking.

"Cheevers, pull over to a gas station!" Mom shouted.

Buford's face was turning colors. Shawn looked terrified. Mom was opening windows.

Cheevers swung the steering wheel sharply to the right. The limo screeched to a stop in a gas station parking lot. Rachel climbed over my lap and bolted out the door.

Buford scrambled out the other side. His right foot stepped on Rachel's sandwich, smashing it into the limo carpet.

"Gross," Shawn said.

Mom made a face. "Cheevers, would you please clean this?"

She and Dad climbed out of the limo and headed into the gas station. I followed Shawn away in the other direction. Buford was running for the men's room.

I could see poor Cheevers slumped over the steering wheel, muttering to himself.

Shawn and I sat on a wooden fence beyond the parking lot. Behind us was a huge, peaceful meadow.

"Where's the brat?" Shawn asked.

I shrugged.

"GET OUT OF HERE!" Rachel's voice screamed through the women's room door.

Buford was standing outside it, looking desperate. "Sorry, someone's in the men's room!" he pleaded.

"Not my problem!" Rachel countered.

Buford bustled toward us. We shot away.

"Some friends," he muttered, hoisting himself over the fence. He walked into the meadow, looking around, red-faced. A few yards away, grazing cattle eyed him warily.

"Nice cows," Buford said. "Very nice. Just give

me a minute in this tall grass. Don't worry, I won't eat it."

Shawn and I cracked up.

But our attention was drawn away from Buford. Just past the limo, a huge RV was pulling away from a gas pump — and beyond it was a gleaming Harley-Davidson motorcycle. An attendant had just gassed it up, but the driver was nowhere to be seen.

"Coooool!" Shawn said.

We walked toward the bike. Cheevers was slipping another attendant some money and pointing toward the carpet.

Shawn ran his fingers along the bike's racing stripes. "Who-o-oa, how'd you like to ride this?"

Rachel skipped over from the side of the gas station. "He'd be too scared to ride it," she said.

"Right, Rachel," I said. "And you wouldn't?"

"I know how to ride one. I saw someone do it in a movie!"

"Hold it! That's a great shot!"

Dad was trotting out of the gas station, holding a few cans of soda. He dumped them into the limo's backseat and pulled out his camcorder. "Go ahead, you two. Climb aboard!"

"*Daaaad*," I moaned.

"Oh, come *on*, it's just a gag," Dad insisted. "You'll thank me when you're older."

"But this belongs to someone," I pleaded.

"I told you he's too chicken," Rachel said to Shawn.

Dad's camcorder was rolling. Mom was spraying the inside of the limo with air freshener. Shawn and Rachel were staring at me.

Great. I could just see Dad's video. Meek Adam, too afraid to climb on a stupid motorcycle. Rachel could blackmail me with the tape the rest of my life.

With a sigh, I threw my leg over the seat and hoisted myself up.

"Yyyyyesss!" Rachel jumped onto the seat, in front of me.

"Hyar, hyar," Dad laughed. "And here are my two little rebels without a cause, revving up — *vroom vroom!* — for one wild and crazy week! Say *hasta la vista*, kids!"

"Pasta la pizza!" Rachel squealed, gripping the handlebars.

I was dying. Absolutely dying. I turned my baseball cap brim-forward to cast a shadow over my face.

"No! No! *No-o-o-o-o-o!*"

Buford's sudden scream made me turn. He was in the field, running toward us, his eyes the size of softballs.

He was not alone.

Chasing him, horns lowered, was a bull!

"Helllp!" Buford tumbled over the fence. He scrambled to his feet, but his pants were falling down around his knees, revealing Bugs Bunny boxer shorts.

With a loud *crrrack!* the bull butted against the wooden fence. It barely held.

"YO!" shouted a deep voice from the area of the men's room. "Get off my hog!"

My eyes darted toward the gas station.

An immense human creature was lumbering toward us, covered with hair and tattoos. He was wearing mirrored sunglasses, but I could tell his eyes were not twinkly.

"Uh-oh," Rachel muttered.

She jerked her wrists forward.

The motorcycle jumped. Its engine roared.

"What are you doing?" I shouted.

"I didn't mean to!" Rachel screamed.

CRACK! went the fence as the bull smashed it to pieces.

"HEEEELLLPPPP!" shouted Buford.

RRRRRRROOOMMMMM! The bike took off.

The biker lunged toward us. His fingertips grazed my ankle. With a loud "ooof!" he fell to the pavement.

"Sto-o-o-o-op!" I yelled.

"I don't know how!" Rachel replied.

We were heading for Dad. He leaped out of the way, landing on the hood of the limo.

I reached around Rachel, grabbed the handlebars, and swerved away.

"Yeeee-hah!" Rachel whooped.

EEEEEEE! The tires screeched.

I held on for dear life and aimed for the road. Out of the corner of my eye, I saw Buford diving into the back of the limo. Cheevers was in the driver's seat. Mom, Dad, and Shawn were scrambling into the back.

"Follow that bike!" Dad commanded.

We zipped onto the highway. The road whizzed beneath us.

"What do I do now?" I yelled.

"Stop yelling in my ear!" Rachel shouted.

"Big help!"

I glanced in the rearview mirror. The limo was gaining on us. Buford's pants were waving out the door like a flag. Behind the limo, the biker was running like a world-class sprinter.

For good reason.

He was being chased by the bull.

6
The Arrival

"*Roll your wrist forward!*" Rachel screamed.
I did. The bike shot ahead even faster.

"*YEEEEAGH!*" I cried. "*Why'd you tell me to do that?*"

"*To scare you!*"

"*Very funny!*"

I fought to keep us going straight. Rachel was bouncing up and down. Horses and cows turned their heads as we zoomed by farmland. Passengers in cars gawked.

I'd had enough. I rolled my wrist back. The bike slowed down.

I leaned to the right and pulled onto a dirt shoulder.

Rachel jumped off the bike and sneered at me. "What'd you do that for? We were just starting to have fun!"

As I climbed off, my knees were shaking. "Rachel, we could have been killed!"

"So?"

"What do you mean, 'so'? I just saved your life!"

"*So?*" She folded her arms and walked away.

Do you understand sisters? I sure don't.

The moment I put the kickstand down, the limo screeched to a halt in the road beside us.

The doors opened and Mom and Dad hopped out. "Oh, my darlings!" Mom cried. "Are you all right?"

"No!" Rachel shrieked.

Mom picked her up. Dad ran over, practically crying. "What's wrong, sweetheart?"

Rachel burst into tears. "Adam's a big party pooper!"

"You've traumatized your sister!" Mom shouted to me.

"She started it!" I said. "She *liked* it!"

"Adam, *really*," Mom said, carrying Rachel into the limo. "We raised you to tell the truth!"

"But — but — Hey, just a minute! Isn't anybody concerned about me?"

"Get in the car!" Dad barked.

I slumped into the backseat, pushing aside the remains of Buford's pants, which were now tattered rags.

Buford was huddled by the other door, his safari jacket spread over his lap. His bare, skinned knees stuck out.

As Cheevers pulled back onto the road, Buford began to shiver. "Uh, excuse me, Mr. and Mrs. Fenster?" he said. "Would you kindly let me retrieve a new pair of trousers from the trunk, or turn down the air-conditioning?"

Behind us, I could hear horns blaring and a loud "YEEEEE-HAHHH!"

I turned and looked through the rear window. Not far behind us, traffic was stopped in both directions. In the middle of the road, the bull was bucking wildly, snorting and kicking its hind legs.

On its back, whooping crazily, was the biker. He was smiling ear to ear.

Well, Buford eventually got his pants and Rachel was treated to an ice cream cone to soothe her trauma.

What did I get? A plate of breaded tofu nuggets on dandelion greens at a place called Reggie's Veggies.

Talk about unfair.

Oh, well. I had to look on the bright side. I figured the worst part of the trip was over.

I was wrong.

The gas station attendant hadn't done a great job. The tuna-banana smell seemed to ferment in the wet, squishy carpet. We were all gagging by the time we reached the next rest stop.

Mom bought a whole bottle of French perfume and dumped it onto the carpet. "Aaah, I love this smell," she said with a smile. "My favorite aunt wore it every day."

Cheevers let the car air out while we walked around the nearby town.

When we saw a big sign proclaiming *Whippleton Welcomes the American Fertilizer Association*, we headed back.

Fortunately, the fishy aroma was gone from the limo. Unfortunately, it now smelled like my great-aunt Lilith.

We were on the road about a half hour when Cheevers announced, "Sixty miles to Mashpea Swamp!"

I almost leaped through the roof with joy.

He drove like crazy. Buford started complaining about his stomach again. (Don't worry. Shawn gave him a look that could stop a wildebeest at sixty yards.)

For the first time all day, I was in a good mood. Then Dad did the one thing I dreaded most. The thing I had hoped he'd never do again.

He started a sing-along.

I don't know about your dad's singing voice, but my dad sounds like a dying water buffalo.

"Ro-o-ow, ro-o-ow, ro-o-ow your boat — come on, everybody!" Dad warbled. "Uh, how does the rest go?"

We all shrugged.

"I know!" Shawn chirped. "Let's play Count the Silos!"

Saved by Shawn. He kept thinking up stupid car games for us to play. Each time we became bored, Dad would start to sing again. Then Shawn would think of another game.

The ideas kind of degenerated after awhile. Counting the nosepickers in other cars, I think, was the low point.

We were in the middle of Name That Roadkill when Cheevers cried out, "Dreamworld sighted!"

We all shut up and plastered our faces to the window.

The first thing we saw was a roller coaster. It was enormous, rising over the tops of gently swaying palm trees. Next we spotted the Ferris wheel and merry-go-round.

Cheevers drove us through an ivy-covered stone archway. Above it, a sign proclaimed:

DREAMWORLD
RESORT FOR SENIORS
SEMPER VIVATE!

"You have to know Greek in this place?" Dad asked.

Rachel rolled her eyes. "It's *Latin*, Dad. It means 'Live forever.' "

"How do *you* know that?" I asked.

"She's not as stupid as she looks," Buford remarked.

"I hate you both!" Rachel snapped.

As Cheevers drove into a parking lot, Mom said,

"Is it my imagination, or did that sign say, 'For seniors'?"

"Well, uh, yeah, I guess," I said. "But, you see, Buford thought I could pass —"

"*I* thought?" Buford retorted. "This was a joint decision, Fenster!"

"I'm sure they're flexible, Mrs. Fenster," Shawn said. "I mean, we couldn't find any place specifically for seventh-graders, and Adam's kind of big for his age —"

Rachel burst out in hysterics. *"Big for his age? You idiots, not *that* kind of senior! Look!"*

She pointed out the window.

I could see the line at the roller coaster. A group of bird watchers with binoculars. Some guests lounging around a pool. Tennis players.

They all had one thing in common.

White hair.

The youngest one must have been about sixty.

Rachel was howling. "You thought this was for high school seniors? This is a resort for senior *citizens!*"

Dad was gaping. Mom's face was bone white. Buford and Shawn were both trying not to laugh.

Me? I was sinking slowly toward the moist carpet.

7
Rhadamanthus Binglehausen

"**A**dam, I believe you have some explaining to do!" Dad thundered.

"It was a mistake, Dad. I blew it. Guess we'll have to go to Disney World after all, huh?"

The veins on Dad's forehead were bulging. "Those reservations have been canceled!"

"Dear, watch your blood pressure," Mom said. "Let's get a refund, then drive back and visit those nice places we passed by — the cheese factory, the Upholsterers Hall of Fame, the plastic kitchenware pavilion . . . "

Shawn and I shot each other a look. For a moment — just a moment — I considered staying.

Dad was already pushing the door open. "I'm going to have a word with the —"

"Who-o-oa! Pardon meeeee!"

An old-timer rolled by on a skateboard, banking sharply toward the roller coaster.

Looking both ways, Dad stepped out. The rest of us scrambled out after him.

We walked toward the parking lot entrance. Just beyond the main road was a tan stucco building. A sign over its front door said *Dream Center*.

At the road, a trim, elderly man dressed in a tank top and shorts held up his hands toward us and blew a whistle. "Runners coming through!" he warned.

We waited. A few dozen old folks dashed by us, their Reeboks and Nikes pounding the pavement.

"Whoa, those geezers are booking!" Buford said.

"They're on their twenty-sixth mile," the old man informed us.

Dad chortled. "You *can't* be serious."

The old man poked Dad in the middle of his pudgy belly. "See you on the track this week?"

"Well, I — I'll have you know — in my day —"

"Go ahead, young fellow," the man said, signaling us to cross. "Before a geezer runs you over."

Dad humpfed and fumpfed all the way to the Dream Center. He pushed the front door open, stomped through the lobby, and barged into a room marked *Director*.

"I demand a refund, due to the deceptive marketing practices of your resort!" Dad roared.

The room was dimly lit. Behind a small, cramped wooden desk with claw feet, a man peered up from behind a pile of papers. His skin was wrinkled and papery, and a scruffy gray beard hung practically to the desk. His bald head shone dully, and the silver hair at the sides was pulled back into a ponytail.

He stroked his beard, casting his slate gray eyes from one of us to the other. "You are not our usual guests," were his first words.

I recognized the voice right away from my phone conversation. "Mr. Dinglehosen?" I said.

"Binglehausen." He rose from his seat and extended his hand to Dad. "Rhadamanthus Binglehausen at your service."

"Um, sir, it's me, Adam, the guy who made the reservation," I blurted out. "You might not recognize my voice because I disguised it —"

Mr. Binglehausen was running around, clearing papers off chairs and a sofa. He moved incredibly quickly, with the energy of a kid.

"Sit," he said.

As we did, he leaped over his desk and landed squarely in his seat.

"Yyyyes!" he said. "You'll excuse me. I've been perfecting that move for years."

"Majorly weird," Buford muttered to me.

"Well, as I was saying," I barreled on, "see, I thought this was a resort for high school seniors and —"

Mr. Binglehausen let out a cackle. "Oh, that's rich! I hadn't heard that one before. Well, not to worry, Adam."

I let out a sigh of relief.

"So, we can have our money back?" Dad asked.

"I didn't say that," Mr. Binglehausen replied. "I'm sure we're equipped to handle your family —"

"Uh, no," I said. "No no no no no."

"I think there's a hotel near the cheese factory," Shawn piped up.

"I can take the bus back," Buford said.

"Pipe down!" Dad bellowed.

"You see, this is Dreamworld," Mr. Binglehausen went on. "I'm in the business of dreams, Mr. Fenster. Anybody's welcome and anything's possible."

"Yes, but the sign says *seniors*," Dad said.

Mr. Binglehausen smiled. "The young have time. They can realize their desires all by themselves. They don't usually need me. The old aren't so lucky. So they come here. However, that doesn't mean I can't help you. Let me give you a brochure."

He held out a leaflet, and Dad began reading it.

"Uh, time out," I said. "I call a family meeting."

We all filed outside Mr. Binglehausen's office.

I shut the door behind us. "Okay," I whispered. "This is a no-brainer, right? The guy's weird. The place is creepy. I vote we go home. I don't care if we forfeit the money. I'll give up my allowance for the next thirty years if I have to. Are we agreed?"

"Agreed," Shawn said.

"Last one to the car is a rotten onion," Buford added.

"I don't know," Rachel said, "I kind of like it here."

"You would," I snapped.

"It does have a nice feeling," Mom added.

"And the facilities are good," Dad said. "Besides, Mr. Binglehausen told me over the phone that he'd sell me the place."

"That was me!" Buford blurted out. "I was disguising my voice!"

I thought my dad would break his neck. Instead, he just shook his head and said, "You got us in quite a muddle, Adam. But we're here already . . . "

"NO-O-O-O-O-O-O!" wailed Shawn, Buford, and I.

"YE-E-E-E-ES!" shouted Dad, Mom, and Rachel.

Mr. Binglehausen peeked out of his door. "Have you reached a decision?" he asked brightly.

"We'll get our bags," Dad said.

My room smelled of mothballs.

What was worse, Shawn and Buford had gotten there first and claimed both beds. I had to sleep on the foldout couch.

We hardly said a word as we unpacked. Then

47

we slumped downstairs for our introductory guided tour of Dreamworld.

Dad, as usual, videotaped everything. We passed pickup basketball games, tennis matches, ultimate Frisbee games — all played by incredibly fit grandparents.

My self-esteem was down around my toes.

All I wanted to do was eat.

At the edge of the resort, the pavement ended at a dark, misty swamp. Gnarled, moss-covered trees sagged of their own weight, and a gassy smell strengthened as we came closer A sign warned *Do Not Pick Berries or Fruit*.

"To our right is the famous Mashpea Swamp," the guide said. "It is a fragile ecosystem, and its vapors are said to have great health benefits. Hundreds of years ago, the aged and infirm would take long walks in here and return cured of their ailments."

Puh-leeze.

As we trudged along, I spotted a funny-looking bush with red fruit the size of strawberries. Hundreds of them drooped low, firm and ripe, gleaming in the setting sun.

I was beginning to drool. I reached out to grab some.

"I'm tellllling!" Rachel said. "Mo-o-o-om!"

"Adam, stay with the group!" Mom said.

I threw a berry at Rachel. It missed and hit Dad.

"Hey!" he shouted.

I was batting zero.

I wanted to go home.

8
Day One

"**A**nd-a-one! And-a-two! And-a-step-kick-hop!" It was Sunday morning, our first full day at Dreamworld. Mr. Binglehausen had drawn up a daily plan for me, with five "periods."

First period was aerobics.

My instructor looked like Granny Clampett on *The Beverly Hillbillies*. She danced around the front of the room to an old Madonna song.

I was in the back row of my class. I was trying to hide. But every wall was a mirror, so I couldn't even escape the sight of myself.

I looked like a pumpkin in a field of stringbeans.

My Hopnoodle Hornblowers T-shirt was dark with sweat. My belly was lapping over the top of my shorts. I was huffing and puffing like Thomas the Tank Engine.

The old man to my right was matching the instructor, step for step. He was also singing along. To my left, a white-haired woman kept saying, "Get down and funky, baby."

Me? I wanted to get down, all right. Get down on the floor and sleep.

I was a mess. I was so exhausted I could hardly breathe. I kicked when I should have stepped. I hopped when I should have kicked. Every time I had to spin, I ended up crashing into the mirror.

At first I was afraid I'd crush some poor old lady. Now I was worried I'd give myself a heart attack.

"Now let's do those hip thrusts!" Granny Clampett yelled. "To the left!"

Hip thrusts?

All around me, the old folks were gyrating and whooping it up. "Come on, young man!" the instructor shouted.

My face was burning. Moving my hips felt like launching an ocean liner. I caught a glimpse of myself in the mirror and thought Barney had wandered into the room by mistake.

"To the right!" Granny commanded.

That was when I saw Dad. Standing in the doorway, bopping to the wrong beat, pointing his camcorder straight at me.

I did the only thing I could think of. I pulled my shirt over my head.

"To the left!" Granny called out.

I spun blindly. I tried to peel my shirt off my face so I could see, but it was too sticky and wet. Someone bumped me from behind. I stepped forward. My foot clipped someone's heel. I lurched sideways.

With a loud *whump*, I landed on the wooden floor.

Madonna kept singing. The oldsters kept dancing.

And Dad — my dad, who claims to love me — was cracking up in the doorway.

I thought the class would never end.

But that was just the beginning. Afterward I had to go to a weightlifting session at the gym.

On the way, I passed Shawn and Buford. "Where are you going?" I asked.

"To the roller coaster," Shawn said.

"How come *you* don't have to suffer?"

Buford signaled me to come closer. He reached into his safari jacket and slipped me a Hershey bar. "Don't tell me I never gave you anything."

Off they went to a day of fun.

I was about to eat the chocolate when Mom and Rachel came racing around the gym. I stuffed it in my back pocket.

"We're going to the pool!" Rachel squealed. "Bye!"

"Rrrrammpf," I grunted (more or less).

I inched my way to the gym as slowly as I could.

Luckily the place was bright and air-conditioned. My personal trainer's name was Clyde. His arms were like toothpicks and his chin dangled like a turkey wattle.

"Okay, young fella," he creaked, "I'll show you how to work the bench press."

The barbell was loaded with weights. I panicked. No way was that little dude going to survive that thing. "That's okay," I said. "I know how. You just spot me."

I lay on the padded bench and jerked the barbell off its metal cradle. I lifted it, arms extended high.

"Not bad!" Clyde said.

I smiled.

WHOMP! Down came the weight on my chest.

I felt as if a house had landed on me. The wind rushed out of my lungs in a big "Whoooof!" I saw stars.

"Oopsy daisy!" said Clyde.

When my vision cleared, he was holding the barbell chest-high in his bony left hand. He extended his right toward me. "You all right?"

"F — f — fine," I rasped. As I sat up, panting, I felt something soft and sticky underneath me.

"What's that chocolate smell?" Clyde asked.

Ugh. It just wasn't my day.

By the time Clyde was finished with me, my knees creaked, my elbows couldn't move, and my thighs felt as if crocodile jaws were clamped around them.

"You did fine, for a start," Clyde said as I left. "We'll increase your weights next time. And keep those chocolates out of your back pocket! Heh heh!"

"Thanks," I mumbled.

I shuffled slowly out of the gym and across the grounds. Next period was lunchtime. To my right, across the green, campuslike lawn, I could see Shawn and Buford riding the roller coaster, laughing and shouting.

To my left, Dad was videotaping Mom and Rachel at miniature golf.

I was going to wave, but I couldn't lift my arm.

Oh, well, I had forty-five minutes to eat. Maybe I could drown my agony in carrot-parsley juice.

After lunch was my recreation period. That meant a stroll to the Dreamworld Common with my family to view the Sunday festivities.

An elderly oompah band, dressed in knickers and feathered green hats, was playing this horrible corny music, while the guests danced on the grass.

"I haven't heard a polka band in years!" Mom gushed.

"Go ahead, Adam and Rachel," Dad insisted, "cut a rug for the camera!"

Cut a rug? I could barely move. Besides, the music was awful. "I guess these guys don't rap, huh?" I asked.

"Why?" Mom asked. "Did you buy a present?"

"*Rap*, Mom, not *wrap!*" I said.

Fortunately the band oomped their last pah right then. A guy took the mike and announced:

"Thanks, all you young whippersnappers out there."

The whole place laughed as if it were the funniest thing ever said.

"And now, for your viewing pleasure, a preview of this year's bathing suit collection!"

"Uh, we don't have to watch this, do we?" I asked.

Even Dad wasn't thrilled by the idea. "Let's partake of the crafts tent," he said.

A wooden statuette of Popeye was on the first crafts table we came to. Behind it, an old dude called out, "Step right up, have your likeness whittled in wood!"

"That's quite good," Dad said. "Sit for him, Adam."

"Do I have to?"

Dad started videotaping. I slumped into the chair opposite the whittler. "Nice to see some fresh faces here," the guy said. "How old are you?"

"Thirteen," I said.

"How old are *you?*" Rachel asked him.

"Rachel, that's not nice," Mom said.

"One nineteen," the whittler said matter-of-factly.

Dad winked at Rachel. "He thought you were asking the price," he said with a chuckle.

"I can hear perfectly well, sir," the man said. "I know, I don't look a day over eighty, eh?"

Dad began angling around us with his camcorder. "I like a good sense of humor. Har har."

But the whittler wasn't laughing at all.

Neither was I when he finished his . . . whittle (or whatever it's called). I looked like Popeye with a potbelly.

"Uh . . . nice," I said. "Thanks a lot."

"I'm working on my skills," he said. "I started at age ninety-seven, after I came here and regained my eyesight."

"Eyesight," I repeated. "Right."

"Everyone still looks a bit like Popeye to me, but I'm getting better."

I grabbed my statuette and bolted. Mom, Dad, and Rachel were heading in the direction of a shuffleboard tournament.

"Can't we go to the roller coaster?" I pleaded.

Dad looked at his watch. "Isn't it time for your track and field period?"

Track and field?

I hated my life. Just hated it.

9
Befogged

"What is this garbage?" Buford said with a grimace.

Buford, Shawn, Rachel, and I were eating dinner together in the Dreamworld cafeteria. Mom and Dad were sitting across the room, at a table for two overlooking the croquet field.

I was half dead. I'd spent most of track and field on my back, panting for breath. Now I was sitting with a date-molasses-prune loaf on my plate. Rachel was happily wolfing down a tuna fish-and-banana on rye. I was trying not to gag.

"What garbage, Buford?" Shawn asked.

"This garbage." Buford opened his mouth wide. Slimy, half-chewed chunks of grayish-green glop coated his tongue.

"Ewwwww!" Rachel shouted.

"That's potato leek stew," I informed him.

Buford spit it into his cloth napkin and began gagging. *How could you let me do that?* I'm dying! I ate a leek!"

He grabbed a water glass and downed the water in one gulp.

"So what?" Rachel asked.

"So what?" Buford repeated. "Have you ever seen one? They look like slugs and they stick to your skin and suck your blood!"

"Those are *leeches*, turnip brain!" Rachel said.

"Oh." Buford opened his napkin over Rachel's plate. "Want mine?"

"Mo-o-o-om!" Rachel screamed, running across the room.

Buford leaned over the table. "Okay, we have about thirty seconds," he whispered. "Let's plan our escape."

"Are you crazy?" I said. "We can't *escape!*"

"Not for good," Buford retorted. "Just tonight. For fun. I did some exploring in Mashpea Township."

"There's a Mashpea Township?" I asked.

"I snuck out of Dreamworld this afternoon to find it," Buford said. "A guard tried to stop me, but I pretended I was feeble-minded."

"That must have been easy," I said.

"Keep it up, Fenster," Buford snarled, "and you can kiss good-bye my entire stock of Snickers and Heath Bars and Cheez Doodles I bought at the Mashpea A & P."

"Sorry," I said.

"How do you expect us to sneak out?" Shawn asked. "First of all, Adam and I don't look as stupid as you. Second, we're all supposed to go to a fifties party tonight."

"Fine, no problem," Buford snapped. "You guys go. While you're jitterbugging with eighty-year-olds in jeans and T-shirts, I'll be exploring the swamp."

"The swamp?" I said. "I thought you wanted to go to the town!"

"No way," Buford said. "The swamp is cooler. We can eat junk food and explore."

Before I could answer, Rachel started tapping me on the shoulder. "Mom says you have to apologize to me or you can't go to the party tonight!"

"Gee, I'm so sorry, Rachel." I sneaked a hunk of date-molasses-prune loaf into my palm. Then I held out my hand, palm down. "Let's shake on it."

Rachel gave me a look. "Shake? We never shake hands!"

"Hey, we have to mature sometime," I said.

The loaf was melting. Shawn and Buford had seen my sleight of hand and were trying not to laugh.

"Well . . . okay." Reluctantly, Rachel reached out for my hand.

Then, with a lightning-quick motion, she pushed it up into my face.

"YEEEEEUCHHH!" I screamed.

"Gotcha!" she yelled, running out of the cafeteria.

Shawn and Buford were on the floor, laughing.

So were all the geezers in the whole place.

I felt about two inches tall.

Getting out of the Fifties Fling was no problem. We waited until Rachel and my parents were flailing away to an Elvis Presley song, then quietly ducked out.

"Whoooo! Boys' night out!" Buford hollered as we ran out of the building.

The grounds were empty. As we sprinted across pools of streetlamp light, crickets cheeped loudly and sprinklers swished water across the lawns.

At the edge of the swamp, we stopped. Buford had brought along three flashlights, and he handed them out.

Three wooden signs faced us. They were small and hand-painted, barely noticeable. One said *Who Dreams, Risks*. The second said *Who Risks, Receives*. The third said *Enter at Your Own Risk*.

I hadn't remembered seeing them the day before. I was going to ask Shawn and Buford if they had, but they were already walking into the swamp.

Buford was looking at his watch. "It's now ten after eight. We'll give ourselves a half hour, then check back and see if they sent a search party."

As Buford walked ahead, the mist rushed up from beneath him like ghostly tendrils. He seemed to float above the ground, blending into the wispy whiteness.

"That's not scary," Shawn said. "Is it?"

"Nahhh," I agreed.

We stood there, frozen. Buford was now invisible.

"Sh-sh-sh-sh-should we get help?" Shawn squeaked.

"What are you waiting for, you chickens?" Buford's voice called out.

I gulped. Shawn's face was dripping with sweat. We stepped further into the swamp.

Squish . . . squish . . . squish . . .

Our footsteps sounded dully on the moist, spongy ground. Gnarled trees peeked through the thickening mists, then seemed to vanish. Spiny plants reached upward like fingers. The red berries on the bushes seemed black.

"This place gives me the creeps," Shawn said.

"Hey, Shawn?" I whispered. "What happened to the crickets?"

"What crickets?"

"That's what I mean. They were so loud a minute ago. Now they're —"

"YOOOOU HAVE ENNNNTERED THE SWAAAAMP ZONE!"

I almost jumped out of my clothes. Shawn screamed.

Buford jumped out of the mist, grinning. "Scared you, huh?"

61

"Nope." Shawn's voice was a high-pitched squeak.

"Uh, I hate to interrupt this super fun time," I said, "but has anyone thought about how we're going to get back?"

Shawn's hands were shaking as he ripped a branch off a berry bush. "We could do a Hansel and Gretel thing," he said. "You know, drop these to make a path."

"Duh. What about the hungry forest creatures?" Buford put a berry in his mouth, then spit it out. "I take that back. No sane animal would eat this stuff."

Buford ripped two branches off and handed one to me.

We walked onward, shoulder to shoulder. The mist was so thick we could barely see each other's faces. I was nervous. When I'm nervous, I get hungry. It seemed a little ridiculous for all three of us to be dropping berries. And they did look good.

I began stuffing them into my mouth.

You know what? They tasted great. Buford was crazy. I began scarfing them by the handful.

The deeper we went, the worse the visibility. If I walked close to Shawn, I lost Buford, and vice versa.

Finally I lost them both.

"Uh, guys?" I called out.

My voice was dull and muffled in the cottony mist.

"Hut sut rallson on the rillerah, and soo-it, soo-it, soo-it . . . " sang a strange voice.

"Buford? Don't do this to me!"

I waved my arms frantically. The mist whirl-pooled up from the ground.

I saw footprints. Large ones, that led to my left.

I looked in that direction. A distant yellow light flickered, growing brighter by the second.

"Hut sut rallson on the rillerah . . . " the voice sang.

"Shawn? Buford?"

No answer.

I swept the mist away again, looking for the berries.

But they were gone. Totally gone.

Just my footprints were left.

Mine and the big ones.

I stumbled around. My heart was like a steam drill. What was going on here? Which way was out?

"And sooo-it, soooo-it!"

I began to run. Blindly. The trees seemed to lurch out of the fog. I shouted. My voice was soft, distorted as if I were underwater. My aching legs pumped like mad.

And then something reached up and grabbed my ankle.

I tried to pull free. I wrenched myself to the right.

Screaming, I plunged into the muck.

10
The Voice
in the Swamp

My eyes flickered open.
My left cheek was resting against the soft, mossy ground. An ant skittered by, veering away from my nose.

My head was killing me. I must have conked out. But for how long?

I groaned and sat up. I could see the snaggly root that had tripped me.

"Guys?" I called out.

An owl answered. "Whoooo?"

I looked around for familiar signs. In the soft light of a full moon, the trees cast twisted shadows on the ground. Buford and Shawn were gone, and so was the berry path.

A yellow light shone through some spidery branches to my right. I remembered seeing it before, but now it was much brighter.

"I'll taaaake you home agaaaain, Kathleeeen . . . "

The voice again. Deep and out of tune.

I shot up to my feet. My flashlight was lying on the ground, still on, still working. I grabbed it and got ready to bolt.

But where?

"Acro-o-oss the ocean faaar and wiiiide . . . "

I couldn't help cringing. The singer was horrible. Maybe not as bad as my dad, but close.

The voice was coming from the same place as the light.

I shone my flashlight on the ground, retracing my path.

A few yards away I saw the large footprints. They veered up a narrow pathway, toward the light and the voice.

I thought about running away. Then I imagined the newspaper headlines in the far-distant future: THIRTY-YEAR-OLD ADAM FENSTER FOUND IN SWAMP! LOST FOR SEVENTEEN YEARS! REJOICING PARENTS ORDER HIM TO CONTINUE DIET!

I decided to follow the path.

As I wound closer, a windowless cottage came into view. Its roof was thatched with leaves and branches. Its walls were built of thin logs, strapped together with vines. The yellow light shone from above its front door.

I walked around it. I was hoping to find some kind of opening, so I could peer in.

No such luck.

"The ro-o-o-ose has all but left your cheeeeck . . . " the voice sang.

I stood at the front door. I swallowed hard and knocked.

"I've waaaatched it fade away and diiiie —"

The voice stopped.

Run! a voice shouted in my brain.

"Who is it?"

The owl swooped onto the roof and stared at me. "Whooooooo?" it screeched.

I tried to speak, but my jaw flapped silently.

A lizard slithered across my shoes. I jumped back. My flashlight clattered to the ground.

"Anybody there?" the voice demanded.

The door began to swing open. A bright light blinded me.

POP!

From inside came a sound like a gunshot.

I turned and ran for my life.

11
WF

POP-POP! POP-POP-POP-POP-POP!
I fell to the ground, covering my head.

"Sorry!" I yelled. "Don't shoot! I come in peace!"

"Adam? Is that you?"

I recognized that voice. I slowly pulled my arms down and looked up into a familiar bearded face.

"Mister . . . Beaglenozzle?" I said.

"Binglehausen," he replied with a chuckle. "But you can call me Rhadamanthus, if it's easier. Won't you come in and have some popcorn?"

A warm smell wafted out of the cottage. I should have been drooling, but somehow my appetite was gone.

"Wow, I'm glad it's you," I said as I followed Mr. Binglehausen inside. "I kind of got lost. Listen, I'm real sorry. I know I'm not supposed to be here —"

"On the contrary," Mr. Binglehausen said. "I've been expecting you."

"You have? Why?"

"Something in your eyes, I suppose. With the older ones, it's easier. Almost all of them end up here. Butter, margarine, or plain?"

"Butter, I guess."

I could barely find a place to walk in the cottage. Books were all over, stacked on the floor and crammed into floor-to-ceiling bookshelves. A narrow footpath wound through them, from the door to the cottage's far corner. There, a stove stood next to a small desk with a computer.

Mr. Binglehausen stood over the stove, buttering the popcorn. "I'm afraid I can't find my chairs under the mess. Go ahead, sit in mine."

"Is this your private hideaway or something?"

"It's where I do my creative work." Mr. Binglehausen chuckled. "And it's not so private. Many of the guests find their way here. At least, the ones who really want to, like you."

"No offense, but I found this place by mistake." I crouched and looked at his computer screen, which was covered with all kinds of strange formulas and numbers. "Cool. Do you have Myst?"

"Not inside. I keep the door closed."

"No, I mean . . . never mind. Can I play around with this?"

"I suppose so. Usually my visitors are not computer literate. I do the work for them."

"What work?"

"The dream work, of course. That's my business."

"Right. I forgot."

The guy was bonkers. But he seemed pretty harmless. And he could get me back to the resort. Eventually.

I pressed escape. The screen blanked out, then a Windows-type menu appeared, with a few icons. I read aloud the labels under them. " 'Payroll . . . Guest list . . . WF . . . ' What's WF?"

"Wish Fulfillment," Mr. Binglehausen replied. "Salt?"

"Sure." I clicked on WF and two more icons appeared. " 'Semper Vivate . . . Other.' "

"Oh, dear, stay away from the first one," Mr. Binglehausen said. "That's what I use for the elders."

I clicked on Other. Mr. Binglehausen set the popcorn on the desk. "This is so wonderful. You're doing my work for me. By the way, how did you enjoy the yucci fruit?"

"You mean the berries? They were great. How did you know I ate them?"

"If you hadn't eaten them, Adam, you wouldn't be here."

I looked at him blankly. "Excuse me?"

The computer beeped. On the screen, a slowly spinning image formed. An image of a head, arms, legs, and a huge torso . . .

The breath caught in my throat. "That looks like me!"

Mr. Binglehausen nodded. "I recently debugged the program. It was making everyone look like Popeye."

Above my image were these words:

SCULPT MODE ON.
TOGGLE FOR AGE MODE.

"What the — ?" I mumbled.

"Click on Sculpt," Mr. Binglehausen said.

I did. The screen read:

SIZE? WEIGHT? BOTH?
INCREASE? DECREASE? OTHER?
SPEED? DELIMITING PARAMETERS?

"Play around a bit," Mr. Binglehausen suggested.

"Cool!" I clicked on Weight and Decrease.

The image's pot belly began to shrink.

I felt as if someone were squeezing the wind out of me. I sprang up.

My pants fell down. I grabbed them and pulled them up to my waist.

Or what was left of my waist. It was smaller now. Smaller than it had ever been.

"What *is* this?" I said.

Mr. Binglehausen roared with approval, clapping his hands. "It works! Go ahead, try some other options."

This was way too creepy. Bizarre. I had to be imagining it.

I grabbed the mouse. "Um . . . I kind of want to be back to normal now."

Mr. Binglehausen looked disappointed. "Oh?"

My hands were shaking violently. The cursor was jumping all over the place. I started clicking at random.

The image expanded, contracted, shrank, grew. I was bobbing up and down. I felt as if I were being pummeled.

Somehow I managed to click on the word Slow. Finally I felt normal.

I backed away, slipping on all the books. "Well, uh, it's been nice, Mister . . . Mister . . . "

I didn't finish the sentence. The moment my feet touched the doorsill, I was going, going, gone.

12
The Escape

"YEEEEEEEAAAAAAGHHHHHH!"

I flew out of the cottage, screaming. The woods rushed by in a hazy dark gray whirl. My feet stumbled on the soft, scrubby soil.

When I hit the ground, I blacked out for a moment.

"Adam?" A voice echoed in my confused, half-alert brain.

"Leave me alone!" I yelled. "You're messing with my mind! Mom! Dad! He-e-elp!"

"What did I do?"

It wasn't the voice of Mr. Binglehausen.

My eyes slowly focused. "Shawn?" I said.

The swampy mist was back. Shawn was leaning over me, looking totally confused.

Buford emerged from the whiteness, hands on hips. "What's he screaming about?"

"I don't know," Shawn said.

"Where were you guys?" I demanded.

"Right here," Shawn replied.

"The whole time?"

"Well . . . yeah. It's only been a few seconds."

"Right. Very funny, Shawn. Ha ha. It must have been *sooo* hilarious to ignore me when I was in need, screaming my lungs out. To sit there laughing while I was abducted into cyberspace and morphed into unrecognizable shapes —"

"Uh, Earth to Adam," Buford said. "Come in for a landing. Time to return to base."

"Adam," Shawn said patiently, "you had a bad fall. Maybe you hit your head. We need to find our way back. Come on."

I stood up. A trail of berries led from my feet into the mist.

"But — but I was just in there —" I pointed in the direction of the lit cottage.

The light was gone.

"Okay, you can't see in the fog," I said. "But these footprints will take us —"

I walked back to where the path had been. But now it was soft and overgrown. The footprints weren't there.

Buford was circling his index finger around his right ear. "Hoo, boy. Must be something in those berries. Get this dude into bed."

"It *was* the berries!" I blurted out. "That's what Fingermuzzle said!"

Adam took my right arm, Shawn my left. "We won't let you fall this time," Shawn said.

Buford pulled a Heath bar out of his safari jacket and handed it to me. "This'll make you feel better. It was a mistake to come out here. I never should have let Shawn talk me into it."

"*Me* talk *you* into it?" Shawn shot back.

As they argued, I stuck the candy bar in my side pocket.

I had no desire to eat it. None at all.

We followed the berry trail back through the swamp. At the end, we stepped up onto the black-top walkway.

I could see the lights of the Fifties Fling flashing through the distant cafeteria windows. We were in luck. I figured the party would be over by now. I expected to see police cars roving over the grounds, looking for us.

I checked my watch. It said 8:17.

"Shawn, what time did you go into the swamp?" I asked.

"Ten after eight," he replied.

Seven minutes? That was impossible.

Unless . . .

I shivered.

Could it have been a dream — the cottage, Mr. Binglehausen, the computer?

"It all seemed so real . . . " I mumbled to myself.

"Huh?" Buford said.

Shawn was already running toward the cafeteria. "Come on, before we get in trouble!"

I didn't move. I was staring at the swamp. At the misty, gray emptiness that crept up to the walkway's edge.

"What happened to the signs that were here?" I asked.

"Huh?" Buford repeated.

"The signs, about risking and dreaming and stuff."

Buford grabbed my arm. "I'm worried about you, Fenster. Dr. Buford says take five candy bars and go to bed. Come on."

We met up with Shawn in front of the cafeteria. But the idea of going back to the party was making me sick. I was exhausted, and I had to wake up bright and early for another day of torture.

"Guys," I said, "I'm going to bed."

"Me, too," Shawn agreed.

"No way!" said Buford. "The night is young. Let's do something fun, like trash the miniature golf course."

I yawned. "Some other time."

"I'll tell your parents we're heading back," Shawn said. "You go ahead."

As I walked back to our room, Buford slumped along beside me. "Wimps," he mumbled.

It took a long time to fall asleep that night. My body felt kind of cramped and tingly. I woke up about three times, curled up in the middle of the bed. Each time, my head was way off the pillow and I had to shimmy back up.

The next morning, Shawn's voice woke me from a deep slumber.

"Adam?" he called. "Where'd you go?"

I rolled over. My entire body was tangled up in sheets, including my face. I flailed around, but I couldn't find daylight. It was as if the entire Dreamworld linen closet had been dumped on my bed.

"Hey!" I shouted. "Is this some kind of joke?"

"Adam?" Shawn called again. "Was that you? Are you hiding? Come on, Buford just snuck off for the supermarket. You can still catch him if you want something special."

Finally I squirmed to the edge of the bed and fell.

And fell.

And fell.

I landed so hard I thought I'd cracked a rib.

When I managed to peek out of the sheet, my heart stopped cold.

Shawn was staring down at me, open-mouthed. He was holding a rolled-up magazine in his hand, as if he were about to swat me.

Have you ever watched a movie from the front row? The characters' faces are so humongous and distorted, you don't even know where to look. Well, that was Shawn.

He was enormous. His tonsils looked like punching bags, his eyes like weather balloons.

Next to me, the sofa bed resembled the White Cliffs of Dover. The sheets I had just climbed out of? They weren't sheets. They were my pajamas.

"What . . . " I said under my breath. "What happened to me?"

"You . . . you . . . shrank," Shawn squeaked.

Then he fell to the floor in a dead faint.

It felt like an earthquake.

13
Small Matters

"Shawn?"
I tried to stand up but I couldn't. My pajamas were weighing me down. They were like a collapsed circus tent.

I wriggled out of them. I stood in the middle of the room in my birthday suit.

Great. Now what?

Under the bed, I spotted a sock with a hole in the heel. It was about the right size to fit around my body. I crawled into it and pushed my head through the hole.

The smell almost knocked me out.

I stood up. The sole of the sock hung limply down my back, like a hood. The ankle part brushed the floor, like a too-long dress, so I had to lift it when I walked.

I looked like a fool. No, a mini-fool. But I couldn't think of fashion at a time like this.

I stumbled over to Shawn and stood in front of his face. "Yo, Shawn!" I called.

His eyes blinked. Then his lips curled into a sneer. "P.U.! What's that stink?"

The force of his breath knocked me off my feet. I fell to the floor in a tangle of sock material.

"I am not seeing this," I heard him say. "I am dreaming. Adam? *Adam, wake me up!*"

I poked my head through the hole. "You are awake!"

Shawn sat up with a start. "What did you do to yourself?"

"What did *I* do? Great, Shawn, blame me. Just like my parents. It's always my fault. Well, guess what, I woke up this way, okay? You think I like the idea of walking around in an old sweatsock?"

Shawn reached down and scooped me into the palm of his hand. "Wo-o-ow! Adam, this is very, very weird. You're like something out of *The Indian in the Cupboard*."

"Shawn, will you listen to me? Something happened during those seven minutes in the swamp last night. Some kind of time warp, I guess. I found this little cottage with Tinklebowser inside —"

"Binglehausen."

"Whatever. Anyway, he must be some kind of wizard. He waits in there for the geezers to find him. Then he sits down at this computer and asks them what they want."

Shawn let out a sudden cackle. "Right, Adam. The old folks just wander into the swamp, la de da, and oops — 'By cracky, Mildred, a time warp!' "

"It's not funny, Shawn!"

"It makes no sense. First of all, Binglehausen has an office in the resort. Why would he use a cottage —"

"You want *sense?* You're talking to a six-inch-tall thirteen-year-old. *I* don't know! Something to do with dreaming and taking risks. You also have to eat the yucci fruit berries, I guess. It's like a screening process."

"Right. Screening. Yucci fruit. Okay. That's logical. And then what? He shrinks them all?"

"No! He grants their wishes. Don't you see? That's why this whole place is so wacky. Old-timers who run marathons, one-hundred-and-nineteen-year-old whittlers, weight lifters with arms like toothpicks — these are not normal people, Shawn. Why do you think they call this place Dreamworld?"

"Wo-o-o-ow," Shawn gasped. "You think he could give me weight-lifter muscles and, like, a little cleft on the chin?"

"*Shawn!*"

"Sorry. I hate to tell you this, Adam, but I think you really blew it. I mean, what's the point of being so small? It's going to be hard to find clothes and —"

"*I didn't wish it!*" I snapped. "Look, he let me use the computer myself. I wanted to make myself thinner, but the whole thing was freaking me out so much I kind of messed up. I must have clicked on Size and Decrease."

"Uh-huh, and you set the time parameter for a little too long."

"Time parameter?"

"Yeah. I mean, you were normal height last night. Then we went right to bed, and you woke up small. Which means you're shrinking at a certain rate, over time. It's like those programs in computer class. You set a start time, a rate, and an end time. Remember?"

"Uh, well, I must have been absent that day."

"You *did* set an end time, didn't you?"

"End time?"

Shawn's face turned white. "We have to find Binglehausen now, Adam, before you fade away to nothing."

"We?"

"I'll take you." He carefully set me down on the floor. "First I'll find you some clothes. You stay here. Don't let anybody see you."

He raced into the hallway. I sat down on my sneaker and waited.

When Shawn returned, he had a tiny gingham blouse and a skirt. "Here. Put these on."

"Are you crazy?"

"They're from Rachel's Barbie. It was on her pile of books. I pretended I needed to borrow a

Baby-sitters Club, but I ripped these off when she wasn't looking."

"Doesn't she at least have a Ken?"

"She was playing Dunk the Hunk with him in the sink."

"Dunk the Hunk? What kind of stupid game is that?"

"I don't know. She's *your* sister! Look, it's only temporary. We'll take your real clothes with us. The minute you grow to normal size, you can change."

"Well, all right. We just better make this fast."

I grabbed the outfit and began slipping it on under the sock. I was smaller than the doll, but the clothes barely fit. Grunting, I snapped the waist shut and buttoned the shirt. Then I pulled off the sock and threw it on the ground.

Shawn burst out laughing. "HOOOO-HA-HA-HA-HA!"

"Knock it off! You're supposed to be my friend —"

"What's so funny?" Rachel's voice called out.

Shawn snatched me up in his hand. His big, warm, fleshy fingers closed around me, cutting off my air supply.

"Nothing," I heard him say.

"Which *Baby-sitters Club* book did you borrow?" Rachel asked.

"Uh, the yellow one," Shawn replied.

"You did not! It's still there!"

I pushed against his palm, trying to open a pocket of air. Then I heard the door open again and my Dad call out, "Are we ready for another day of fun and fitness?"

Shawn's hand tightened. I felt like a small hot dog in a large bun.

"Where's Adam?" my mom asked.

"At the gym!" Shawn blurted out. "He was so full of energy from his long sleep that he wanted to get a head start on the day. So he ate an early breakfast and —"

"Good morning!" sang Buford's goony voice. "How nice to see everyone."

"Where were you?" Rachel asked.

"Well, er, I was at the . . . gym!" Buford replied. Gulp.

"How's my boy doing?" Dad said.

"Huh?" Buford asked.

"How's Adam doing?" Dad repeated. "You just said you were at the —"

"They . . . must have crossed paths!" Shawn quickly said. "See, Adam wanted to jog first around the resort, and —"

"Adam? Jog?" asked Mom.

"He's changing, Muriel," Dad said. "I knew this would happen."

"Shawn, what do you have in your hand?" Rachel asked.

"Nothing," Shawn answered.

"Let me see."

Shawn's hand jerked to the right. He squeezed tighter. I pushed again, but he wouldn't loosen up.

"Come on, open up!" Rachel whined.

Now Shawn was pulling me violently all over the place. I was gagging. I couldn't breathe.

Finally I did the only thing I could do.

I bit him.

"Yeow!" said Shawn.

I felt myself rising fast, like an elevator. And then Shawn's fingers opened, palm up. Fresh air rushed around me.

I was staring up at my parents, Rachel, and Buford!

14
Shawn to the Rescue

I froze.

Mom, Dad, and Buford were blabbering on about breakfast. Rachel, however, was staring right at me.

She looked absolutely horrified.

"Pretty good, huh?" Shawn said. "That whittler is getting better and better!"

Mom and Dad turned to look, then Buford.

I tensed every single muscle and held my breath.

"It's a very good likeness," Dad said.

"Not at all like Popeye," Mom added.

Buford nodded. "Uglier than Adam, though. Fatter and dumber-looking, too. But why is he wearing a dress — ?"

"GIVE ME BACK MY BARBIE CLOTHES, YOU CREEP!" Rachel shrieked.

"No!" Shawn closed his fist around me again. "I — I had to take them, Rachel. You see, the whittler's seamstress wasn't done with the outfit, and Adam didn't want anyone to see his statue naked. He's funny that way —"

"GIVE THEM TO ME! YOU STOLE THEM!"

I was lunging back and forth in the darkness.

"Rachel, stop pulling his arm!" Mom commanded.

"All right, Rachel!" Shawn said. "I'll give them to you."

That's what he thought! I bit him again.

"Yeouch!" Shawn said.

"What are you yeouching about?" Rachel asked.

"Splinters!" Shawn snapped. "Look, Rachel, Adam swore me to secrecy, but I guess I can tell you. See, he insisted the seamstress make you a special handmade Barbie outfit for your birthday —"

"But my birthday's in October," Rachel said.

"He knew that! But, uh, you see, the lady's kind of nearsighted, and she said it'll take until October if we can get her a sample right now."

I was cringing. That was the dumbest excuse I had ever heard in my life.

"Can she make it an oyster-hued collarless jacket with loop closures, and a matching pair of elastic-waisted black-and-cream striped georgette pants?" Rachel asked. "It's, like, the only outfit Barbie's missing."

"That's *exactly* what Adam had in mind!" Shawn replied.

"It *is?*" Rachel asked.

"What a sweet brother," Mom said.

"Who taught him about clothes?" Dad muttered.

"He has a hard enough time with matching socks," Buford remarked.

"Well," Shawn said, "Adam is full of surprises these days. Anyway, gotta run. Big day ahead. I'll catch up with you guys at lunch. Bye!"

Now I could feel myself moving. Fast.

"What about breakfast?" I heard Buford yelling in the distance.

Shawn didn't answer. He was booking.

My body was pounding up and down. I was sweating like a pig. And Shawn's palm was beginning to smell like the monkey cage at the zoo.

"Yo, can I have some air?" I called.

"Sorry!" Shawn said. He loosened his grip and let me poke my head above his thumb.

The hallway of the hotel zoomed by. Shawn pushed through the front door and raced across the grounds. I sat tight, admiring the view.

When we got to the main building, Shawn barged right into Mr. Binglehausen's office.

A secretary looked up from his desk. "Excuse me? May I help you?"

"Mr. Binglehausen, please," Shawn said.

The woman frowned. "I'm sorry, young man, but he's not in. He left yesterday for vacation and won't be back until next week."

15
The Return

"*Next week?*" I shouted.

The secretary dropped her pencil. "How did you do that?"

"Do what?" Shawn asked.

"Make that doll speak!"

Shawn turned white. "Uh . . . ventriloquism. Say bye-bye, Adam!"

"Bye-bye, Adam," I squeaked.

Shawn turned and sped away.

"What now?" he asked as he bounced down the stairs.

"The swamp!" I said. "We have to get to the computer."

"But what if he's not there? How does the time warp mechanism work? Can you activate it on your own by eating the berries, or does Mr. Binglehausen actually have to be physically present —"

"I don't know, Shawn!"

"— or is it the combination of the berries and

a very intense wish, like you wanting to lose weight or —"

"Why are you asking me this stuff?"

"I hope you don't have to have, like, big dreams and deep wishes and stuff. I don't have any. I just want to, you know, lead a happy life and not flunk math and look old enough to get into PG-13 movies —"

"*Shawn, heads up!*"

I could see Buford stalking toward us across the lawn.

"Where do you think you're going?" he asked.

Shawn stuffed me into his back pocket. "To the gym," he said.

"*Not!* The gym's in the other direction, space cadet," Buford replied. "Maybe you're looking for Adam, so you two can hog all the candy he stole."

"I don't know what you're talking about, Tut-weiler," Shawn said. "Adam doesn't have your candy, and neither do I."

"Well, who does?"

"I don't know. Here, take some money and buy some more." Shawn stuck his hand in his front pocket.

His pants tightened. His back pocket squished me. My foot was stuck in a wad of stale orange bubble gum. Dust and lint pressed against my face.

"Ahhh . . . ahhh . . . CHOOOO!" I sneezed.

"What was that?" Buford asked.

Shawn sniffed loudly. "Whew, must be my allergies! It's that time of year. Here's some cash."

He pulled his hand out of his pocket. I fell into the gum.

"Thanks," Buford grumbled. "And if you see Rachel, smell her breath for chocolate."

"Right."

I could hear Buford lumbering away. Shawn's hand reached into his pocket and lifted me close to his face. *"Smell her breath for chocolate?"* he whispered.

I felt as if I'd been blasted by poison gas. "Uh, speaking of breath, did you brush your teeth this morning, Shawn?"

"Oops." Shawn pulled me away. "Hey, what feels so sticky?"

"The gum on my foot."

"Yuck!" Shawn opened his hand.

Down I went. "Who-o-oa!"

I grabbed Shawn's pinky at the last minute and hung over the ground. *"Will you be careful?"*

"Sorry." Shawn gathered me up again and headed into the swamp.

Even now, early in the morning, the mist was swirling. Below us, I could make out clumps of shriveled red yucci berries.

"Follow the path," I said. "Slowly."

He trudged through the swamp. I looked around desperately for anything familiar.

Finally the berry trail ended. "This must be

where you fell," Shawn said. "Where's the cottage?"

"There should be a path through some trees further up," I said.

As Shawn started off, I heard the *squish-squish-squish* of footsteps behind us.

"Yo, sneaking off to find the candy, Ferguson?" Buford's foghorn voice sliced through the air.

Shawn groaned. His hand began to close.

"Don't put me back in that pocket!" I said. "Just set me down on the path!"

The moment my feet touched the soil, I ran. At my weight, I could scoot along pretty easily without sinking. I could hear Buford and Shawn arguing, but the fog swallowed their words.

The pathway was right where I'd expected it. The cottage was nowhere to be seen, but this time I could definitely make out footprints beneath me.

Yucci bushes lined the pathway. My mouth started to water. I hadn't eaten anything since the night before, and I was starving.

At my height, the berries were the size of basketballs. Some hung as low as my face. I walked over and took a bite.

Whoa. The flavor was amazing. A hundred times more intense than when I was full height.

I couldn't stop myself. I chomped away until my cheeks bulged and juice slobbered out of my mouth.

When I finally looked up, the mist was whirling around me, picking up speed until it roared. A clump of flying moss beaned me on the side of the head. I had to shove my arms down to keep my Barbie blouse from flying off. I braced myself for a wild ride.

But the wind died down as suddenly as it started. And when it did, the sky was clear.

"Hut sut ralllllson on the rillerah . . . "

I spun around. The cottage stood in a clearing just ahead of me, plain as day, its door wide open.

"Mr. Buglenosen?" I called out.

I heard some bonking and clattering, and the old man stepped out. "My goodness, Adam. What happened to you?"

"Is this where you spend your vacation, in Limboland?" I barged inside the cottage (well, maybe *skittered* was more like it).

"Oh, dear, I suppose I need to work on that WF program, don't I?"

"That would be nice," I said.

Mr. Binglehausen rushed over to the computer, tripping on a pile of books. He sat at the desk and began tapping on the keyboard like crazy. "The trouble is, Adam, I haven't finished that program. I never put in a reverse function."

"That's a joke, right? Ha ha."

But Mr. Binglehausen was sweating very seriously. "Well, you see, most of my programming hours went into Semper Vivate and I'm just not sure —"

"AAAAAAAAAAGH!"

I spun around.

Standing in the door, her fists firmly drawn up to her frightened face, was my sister, Rachel.

16
Sister Act

"Oh, my," Mr. Binglehausen said. "I didn't expect this —"

"Rachel, how did you get here?" I asked.

Rachel's mouth flapped open a few times. Then she cleared her throat and said, *"AAAAAAAAAAGH!"*

"Calm down, please," Mr. Binglehausen said. "Would you like some popcorn?"

"Adam, what happened to you?" Rachel asked.

"Rachel, I think you should sit . . . "

She did, and I carefully explained everything — my trip into the swamp the night before, the cottage, how I messed up the computer.

As I spoke, I had to pull up my skirt. It was coming loose.

"Adam, you're still shrinking!" Rachel said.

"I know. That's why I'm here. How did you find this place, Rachel?"

"I was on my way to the seamstress. Mommy

95

said I could go if I hurried. See, I forgot Barbie needed a pair of strappy slingback sandals. I mean, the jacket and pants were cool, but she couldn't go barefoot. That would work on the beach, but for indoors —"

"*And?*" I interrupted.

"On my way, I saw Shawn running across the field. Without you. It looked like he was trying to find something. I thought about how nervous he was in the room this morning. Then I thought he might be looking for you. Like, you'd run away. Or — or got lost. I —"

She started to cry.

I nearly fainted. Rachel, concerned about me? Up until then, the nicest thing my sister ever said to me in my life was "See you later, sweathog."

"It's okay, Rachel," I said, patting her toe.

"Anyway, then I got lost. So I tried to find my way out, and I saw these berries, and they looked so good —"

Clickety-click-clack-clack! "Okay, here we are . . . " Mr. Binglehausen said.

She stood up and looked at the screen.

"Whoooooa, that looks like you, Adam!"

I climbed up the chair and onto Mr. Binglehausen's lap.

My own form loomed in front of me, outlined in longitude-latitude lines. Sort of like a human body shaped out of a spider web.

Mr. Binglehausen's fingers danced over the

keyboard. Then, with a flourish, he pressed Enter.

"Bingo!" he said, jumping up. "In a minute or two, the calculations will be done! Popcorn for everyone!"

I tumbled off his lap and landed on the floor with a thud. "Ow!"

"Oops, sorry." Mr. Binglehausen put a pot on the stove and fired it up. "Finally I've solved this blasted program. Do you understand what this means, Adam and Rachel?"

"Yeah, I'll grow again," I said.

"I can establish Dreamworld Resort for Seniors *and* Overeaters!" Mr. Binglehausen barreled on. "Then, who knows what other condition I can treat?"

"I have this friend, Buford, who's an infectious dork," I suggested. "Maybe you could —"

"Oops!" Rachel called out.

We both turned. Rachel was kneeling on the chair, holding the mouse. Her face was white as a sheet.

"What happened?" Mr. Binglehausen asked.

"The numbers stopped," Rachel said. "So I started clicking . . . "

"Yes?" Mr. Binglehausen said, pouring oil into the pot. "And you clicked on Reverse?"

"Well . . . I tried to, but I guess I got a little excited." Rachel's voice was a parched whisper. "I pressed Delete."

17
The Sacrifice

"*D*elete?" I yelled. "Delete the *program* or delete *me?*"

TSSSSSHHHH! The oil spattered out of the pot onto Mr. Binglehausen's arm.

"YEEEEOW!" he yelled.

I scurried across the room and leaped onto Rachel's lap.

The hard-drive light was flickering. The screen now read:

SUBJECT TO BE DELETED . . . WAIT . . .

"What do we do now?" Rachel screamed.

"Unplug it!" I yelled.

"You can't!" Mr. Binglehausen replied. "It doesn't run on electricity."

"Oh, I forgot, we're in fairyland here!" I said. "Great! Just great! I'm going to disappear, *pfffft*, in a place that doesn't really exist, because of my stupid sister —"

"I didn't mean it!" Rachel shouted. "I was just trying to help!"

"Rachel, if you delete me, I'll kill you!"

"BUT YOU WON'T BE ABLE TO!" Rachel wailed.

"WELL, AT LEAST YOU'LL GET YOUR BARBIE CLOTHES! I HOPE YOU'RE HAPPY ABOUT THAT —"

Beeeeep!

We turned to the screen. The message had changed:

DELETION INTERFACE PREPARED.
ARE YOU SURE? Y/N

I jumped onto the keyboard's N.
The next message flashed:

CONTINUE? REVERSE?

Rachel grabbed the mouse.

"Don't blow this one!" I said.

She stuck out her tongue and clicked on Reverse.

TO PROCEED, ENTER SACRIFICE:
(F1 FOR MENU OF OPTIONS)

"Sacrifice?" I jumped on the letters *N*, *O*, *N*, and *E*.

PROGRAM ENDING . . .
BYE-BYE!

"No!" Mr. Binglehausen shouted.

Quickly he brought his index finger down on F1. "Adam, this is part of the program. You have to sacrifice something to get your dream."

"Isn't there a song about that . . . ?" Rachel said.

"Oh, please," I mumbled. "This place is turning into the Mickey Mouse Club before my eyes."

The new menu materialized onto the screen:

THE FOLLOWING CHOICES CONSTITUTE SACRIFICE FOR THE SUBJECT. CHOOSE ONE:
1. START VEGETARIAN DIET.
2. DEVELOP STUDY HABITS.
3. KEEP A POETRY JOURNAL.
4. BEGIN OBOE LESSONS.
5. LEARN PLUMBING.
6. GET A PAPER ROUTE.
7. KISS YOUR SISTER.

"EWWWWWWWWWW!" Rachel and I both said at the same time.

"Uh, what's an oboe look like?" I asked Mr. Binglehausen.

"Hello? Hello?" came a distant voice. "Uchhh, my shoes . . ."

Rachel and I froze.

"Dad?" she murmured.

"What's *he* doing here?" I asked.

Mr. Binglehausen put his hand over his face. "I was wondering when he'd show up."

"Officer, where are you?" Dad shouted.

"He brought the police!" Rachel said.

"I can't let him see me like this," I said. "Hide me!"

Rachel wrapped her fingers around me. They were encrusted with bits of Rachel's favorite sandwich material, tuna fish and bananas.

I thought I was going to toss my yucci fruit.

Mr. Binglehausen was now singing that weird song of his — and laughing. "Some help you are!" I shouted.

But Rachel's disgusting fingers muffled my voice.

Now Dad was knocking at the door. "Anybody in here? I seemed to have lost my way —"

I peeked between Rachel's fingers.

Slowly the door swung open.

My eyes shot over to the computer screen. Like it or not, I had one choice.

A wad of crusty tuna-banana was attached to Rachel's knuckle, right in front of my face. I held my breath and moved to one side of it.

I puckered up my lips and fought back nausea.

Then, closing my eyes, I planted a kiss on Rachel's finger.

18
Dreamworld

"*Adam, you are the most disgusting pig in the world!*" Rachel screamed.

Her hand opened. I fell.

My head smacked against the floor. I think I shouted, but I'm not sure.

I do know that I passed out. Because when my eyes opened, I was in the swamp again. The mist was whooshing around me, and my face was smashed against a bush.

Shawn was shaking my shoulders.

"Adam, are you okay?" he asked.

I sat up. The ground was swirling. I was dizzy.

"Yeah . . . " I said, wiping my mouth off. "I guess."

I turned away from the bush. Right away, I noticed two things.

One, I was looking Shawn straight in the eye. We were the same size.

Two, it was dark outside.

"Come on," he said. "Buford's already gone

102

back. Even he's creeped out by this place."

"Wait a minute! Where are Rachel and Dad?"

Shawn looked at me as if I had totally lost my mind. "At the dance!"

"What dance?"

"The Fifties Fling, remember?" Shawn helped me up by the arm. "Man, you must have hit your head really hard."

I stood up, still a little wobbly. "Shawn . . . when we came in here, how *tall* was I?"

"How tall?" Shawn burst out laughing. "Oh, about the size of a pencil."

"I thought so!"

"Uh, *joke*, Adam . . . " Shawn's smile vanished. He put the back of his hand against my forehead. "You're a little warm. Dr. Shawn says, time to go to bed before you scare everyone."

"You mean . . . I didn't go to the cottage?"

"What cottage?"

"I didn't shrink?"

"You *need* a shrink!"

Leaning against Shawn, I limped out of the swamp.

I had been here before. The *last* time I had left the swamp with Shawn and Buford, I also thought I'd been dreaming.

But I *hadn't* been dreaming. I woke up the next morning, shrunken.

Unless . . .

Unless the whole thing was a dream.

My mind was spinning.

The night hadn't happened. I hadn't gone to the cottage. I hadn't shrunk. Everything was back to normal.

For a moment, I was flooded with relief.

Then I realized I had a whole spring break in Dreamworld left to go.

My stomach plunged to my feet. "Uh . . . maybe we should go back in," I said. "Have you tasted the red berries? They're really good."

Shawn gave me a look. "Come on . . . "

Buford was waiting for us on the pathway. He was pacing back and forth, looking at his watch. "It's eighteen minutes after eight!" he announced. "The party's got a good couple of hours to go. Let's do something fun."

With a sneaky smile, he reached into his pocket and pulled out a load of firecrackers. "These would sound good in the miniature golf course."

Shawn pulled me toward the resort. "No way, Buford. You'll get us all kicked out of here!"

My ears pricked up.

"Come on, you chickens!" Buford shouted. "Buck-buck-buck-buck-buck . . . "

Buford jumped over the locked fence of the miniature golf course.

Across the campus, a light went on in an office building. I saw a figure staring out the window, in Buford's direction.

I knew just what to do.

I broke away from Shawn and ran after him as fast as I could. *"Wait for meeee!"* I shouted. *"YEEEEEE-HAAAAA!"*

"Adam, you're crazy!" Shawn said.

"Pipe down, buddy," Buford called from inside the fence.

I saw a match flicker. Buford climbed back over the fence and ran away.

"Hey, what's going on here?" a deep voice called out.

An old guy with a park-ranger-style hat grabbed me by the arm.

KAAAAAA-BOOOOOOOOM!

The miniature golf course lit up. Clods of dirt flew in all directions.

"He did it!" Buford yelled, pointing to me. The guard glared at me angrily.

But I didn't feel bad at all. I leaned back my head and shouted at the top of my lungs, *"SEM-MMMPERRRR VIVAAAATE!"*

Epilogue

Well, I never did have that second day in Dreamworld.

We were kicked out. Just as I'd hoped.

The guard pulled Mom, Dad, and Rachel out of the party. He made all of us march to the office, where he called Mr. Binglehausen.

Mom and Dad were furious. When Mr. Binglehausen came in, they fell all over themselves apologizing.

"I cannot make dreams come true," Mr. Binglehausen said, "if we allow nightmares like your children in our resort."

Dad was really insulted about that. "Buford Tutweiler is not my child!" he said.

If Buford were a dog, he would have had his tail between his legs.

As for me, I watched Mr. Binglehausen like a hawk. I thought for sure I'd catch a wink, a glint in the eye — *something* that would hint about the cottage.

Nada. Absolutely nothing.

He let us stay the night, but we had to be out by nine the next morning.

Dad stopped by our room before he went to bed. With a weary smile, he said, "I'm calling Disney World first thing in the morning. Reservation for five."

I nearly started dancing. Shawn let out a whoop. Buford said, "Excellent idea, Mr. Fenster. In fact, I was going to recommend it myself —"

"After we make one drop-off . . . in Fensterville." He glared at Buford, then ducked out of the room. "Good night, fellas."

" 'Night!" Shawn said.

" 'Night!" I echoed.

As Dad padded down the hallway, I yelled, "YYYYYYESSS!"

This — *this* was a spring break!

Shawn and I exchanged high, low, and every other kind of fives.

Buford was counting on his fingers. "Reservation for five . . . ?"

I plopped into bed. I turned on my side and curled into my favorite sleeping position, with my hands curled up to my mouth.

"Uh, guys . . ." Buford said. "Why is he stopping in Fensterville?"

"Uh, well, Buford," Shawn began. "It's like this . . . "

Me? I wasn't listening.

My eyes were bugged open. I was staring at my fingers.

Wedged into my index fingernail was a furry yellowish thing. Its smell was unmistakable.

It was mostly tuna fish. But it had a trace of banana.

About the Author

Peter Lerangis is also the author of *Spring Fever!* He does not actually live in Hopnoodle Village, although he'd like to visit someday. He does, however, love to eat. If you invite him over, stock up on chocolate chocolate chip ice cream. He will thank you greatly.